Lively Tails of Leo the Lop

A Serendipity™ Book to Color

PRICE STERN SLOAN
Los Angeles

Printed and assembled in Mexico.

In a corner of a forest a whole bunch of bunnies is born.

Leo the Lop is the only bunny whose ears hang straight down.

The other rabbits laugh at Leo every time he walks by.

Leo struggles and strains, trying to make his ears stand up.

He hangs upside down from a tree branch showing his ears which way to go.

A possum joins Leo on the branch and asks him what he is doing.

After the possum tells Leo he is normal, Leo begins to think that the other rabbits are not normal.

The other rabbits try to tie down their ears using rocks and twine.

When that doesn't work, they hang upside down with their ears tied to a branch.

They meet the possum, and he tells them that they are normal..

All the rabbits decide that normal is whatever you are!

In the evening, all the forest creatures begin to fall asleep.

Leo has trouble sleeping because he keeps thinking that he is tiny and cute.

The next morning, he looks in the mirror and decides he wants to be rough and rugged and brave.

At creature school everyone laughs at him except the old gray owl who is the teacher.

The owl asks each of the students to describe the way he looks that morning, and Leo blurts "brave."

All the other creatures laugh, and Leo rushes into the forest in tears.

Leo tries to decide what to do.

Meanwhile, a squirrel smells smoke, and fire spreads through the forest.

All the creatures try to remain calm and decide what to do.

Without a thought for his own safety, Leo runs to rescue his trapped friends.

Leo tells everyone to hold hands and follow him, and he leads them to safety

All the animals cheer for Leo.

The snow brings winter to the forest, while all the animals sleep.

Leo can't sleep because he is bored by having to stay indoors all winter.

He tries making funny faces in the mirror.

He goes outside to find someone to play with.

The squirrels are asleep, but he decides to wake them up.

A very upset squirrel sends Leo flying into a snowbank.

Leo asks the birds to play, but they are busy looking for food.

He sees an old owl who asks him who he is and what he is doing.

The owl explains to Leo that he can have fun just playing by himself.

He has fun sliding down some hills.

Then he builds a big snow bunny.

One day he notices little green shoots sprouting up, and he realizes spring is beginning.

Leo decides to tell all his friends about his great winter.

First he tells Creole about his snow bunny.

Then he comes upon Grampa Lop resting in the forest.

Leo tells Grampa Lop about everything he has done that winter.

The Furry Eyefulls are interested in all Leo has to tell them.

Patti the Caterpillar is just hanging around looking for butterflies.

Leo tells Patti about his wonderful winter.

Even Morgan listens as Leo tells him about all the fun he had that winter.

Berry Hucklebug is too startled to listen to Leo's stories.

Some days Leo would just go off and play by himself.

Leo still has one problem—his ears always hang in his soup.